To Mom and Dad –
thank you for your never-ending love and support

Thanks to Shanti Devi and Monica Gripman-King for initiating the idea of the book *The Tree*, and for connecting me with Illumination Arts. Thanks to my brother Zach Lyons, web gurus Aaron Booker & Brett Lovins, Katey Roemmele, Barbara Connor and Neil Rabitoy at Thresholds and Dr. Frank James. Very special thanks to the entire Illumination Arts crew who have put so much effort into creating this beautiful book. I appreciate how everyone on the Illumination Arts team contributed to *The Tree*'s creation, and it is an honor and pleasure to have you as my new friends. Thanks to Dave Danioth for making *The Tree*'s story come alive in your exquisite illustrations. And finally I'd like to thank "The Tree," the big Douglas fir out in the Quinault River Valley, whose song this book celebrates. Also thanks to the forest in the Twisp River valley for contributing the final verse of *The Tree*.

Dana Lyons

To all mothers –
the givers and unconditional nurturers of life

A grateful thanks to my family, especially my children Carissa and Jaron for their continuous inspiration, to my wife Patricia, to the neighborhood children Johnathan, Meg, Kristin, Matthew, Adam, Cassie, Ricky, Riley and to Aleesha Gibbs for her help in organizing them for a photo shoot, and finally to Dana Lyons, Cheryl Kerry and the Illumination Arts staff – John, Ruth and Arrieana Thompson, Terri Cohlene, Andrea Hurst, Trey Bornmann, Bob Gruber, Cathy Sangster, Necia Velenchenko, Allison Luhrs and Janell Porcolab – for this opportunity.

David Danioth

THE TREE

Written by Dana Lyons
Illustrated by David Danioth

Forewords by Julia Butterfly Hill & Pete Seeger

ILLUMINATION
Arts

PUBLISHING COMPANY, INC.

To further your understanding of the environmental issues reflected in this book, please refer to the following charities:

The **Jane Goodall Institute** advances the power of individuals to take informed and compassionate action to improve the environment of all living things. With Dr. Jane Goodall's words and example as guiding principles, the Institute inspires hope for a brighter future. Contact **www.janegoodall.org** for information.

Only if we understand can we care.
Only if we care will we help.
Only if we help shall all be saved.

Dr. Jane Goodall

The **Circle of Life Foundation**, founded by Julia Butterfly Hill, envisions a sustainable culture that honors biological and cultural diversity. Through education and outreach, the foundation promotes efforts to protect and restore the Earth. It inspires, supports and networks individuals, organizations and communities so together, they can create environmental and social solutions that are rooted deeply in love and respect for the interconnectedness of all life. Contact **www.circleoflife.org** for information.

Foreword by Julia Butterfly Hill

My memories from the time of being a child are filled with playing in forests and climbing trees. During times when I was frustrated, sad, or angry, I remember always searching out trees because they would make me feel better.

Now that I am older and have spent over two years living in the branches of an ancient redwood, I see how trees give us all so many special gifts. Not only do they share with us places to rest when our hearts, bodies, and spirits are tired and worn, but they also provide so many of our actual needs for survival. From clean air to breathe and water to drink, to acting as nature's air conditioners, trees are great teachers of unconditional giving.

Trees and our Earth take such good care of us and all they ask in return is that we do the same for them. This beautiful home we all live on wants to give to us forever. But if we don't take good care of it and if we continue cutting down all the trees, eventually it will have nothing left to give us.

Our Earth needs everyone's help — young and old, boys and girls, all colors, shapes, sizes and abilities. We are all important, and as Dr. Seuss tells us in *The Lorax*,

Unless someone like you cares a whole awful lot,
Nothing is going to get better. It's not.

Things can get better, and they will, as each of us decides to become a caretaker of the trees, the Earth, and each other. We are the ones.

Julia Butterfly Hill
Author of *Legacy of Luna*

Foreword by Pete Seeger

Sixty-nine years ago I went to a school where I learned to use an ax and how to cull out the young trees, as one thins out a row of carrots. I used these skills seventeen years later when my wife and I built a small house in which we raised our three kids. Later on, we could afford to hire carpenters to build a porch for us. They used lumber from a Douglas fir tree.

So now, as I read this beautiful book, I realize I'm a part of the problem, even as I would like to be part of the solution. I know this book is part of the solution. Looking back at the lessons of my youth, I recommend to the kids: Don't let your studies interfere with your education.

Pete Seeger — Musician, Songwriter
Where Have All the Flowers Gone? If I Had a Hammer and *Turn, Turn, Turn*

There's a river flowing near me,
and I've watched that river change and grow.

For eight hundred years I have lived here,
through the wind, the fire and the snow.

I see salmon return every summer.

And I watch young owls learning how to fly.

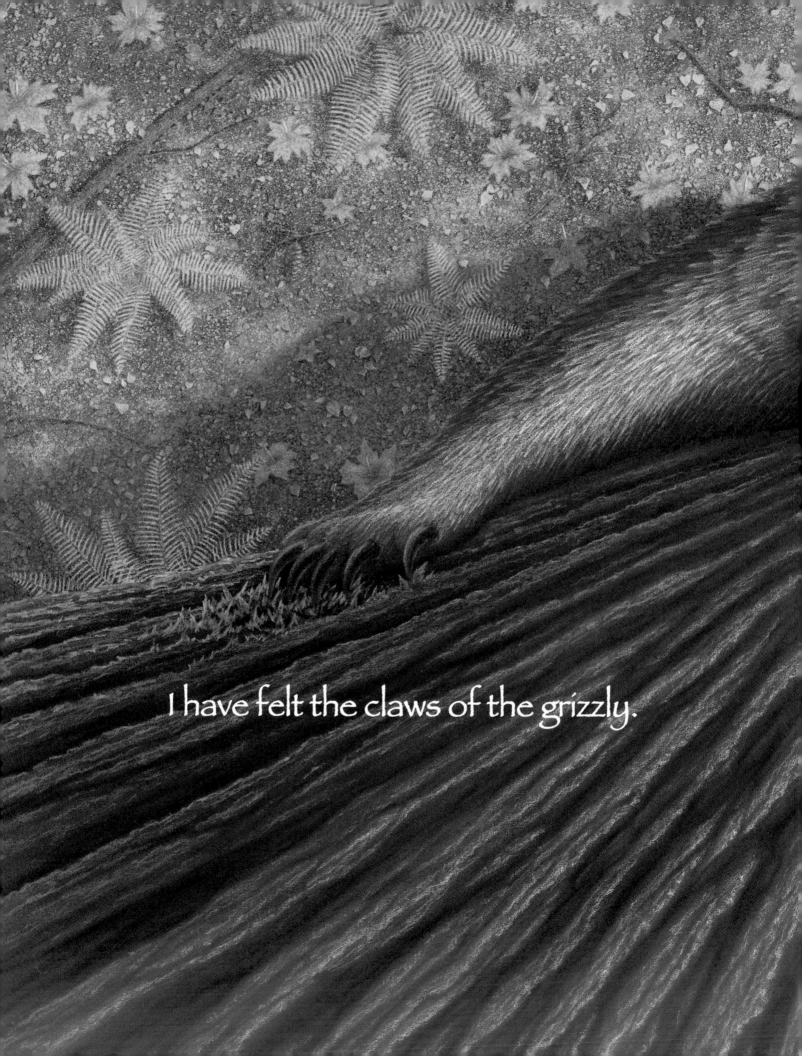

I have felt the claws of the grizzly.

And I've heard the lone wolf's cry.

I have seen great glaciers melting,
and I've met lightning eye to eye.

But now I hear bulldozers coming,
and I wonder, *Am I soon to die?*

Who will house the owl?
And who will hold that river's shore?

And who will take refuge in my shadow,
if my shadow falls no more?

But now I hear children running,
circling my trunk... hands soft and strong.

People are holding on to my branches,

So the wind may always carry my song.

The story of
THE TREE

A few years ago, while recovering from a back injury, I went camping in the Olympic Rain Forest. For four relaxing days I read and played my guitar at the base of an ancient Douglas fir. As I was packing up to return home, a strange thing happened – a fully formed song came flowing through me. Looking up into the giant tree, I said, "I'll bet this is your song."

As the years passed, whenever I introduced *The Tree*, I would tell audiences that the author of the song was a Douglas fir, even though I only half-heartedly believed it myself.

One day on the ferry to Orcas Island, I ran into an old friend. "Are you coming to the celebration?" he asked. "After a ten-year struggle, the Madrona Point burial ground has finally been returned to the Lummi people."

We went together, and after the feast my friend said the tribal chief wanted to hear *The Tree*. As I sang, the elders seemed riveted to each note and word. Later, I told the story of the song's origin and that I had always wondered if it really did come from that ancient Douglas fir.

"It did," said the chief. "I recognize the tune." He then explained, "It is known in our tradition that each tree has its own song. Our music comes from them. We show our respect for the great trees by singing their songs and playing them on the flute. We must all work to save the ancient groves in our territory."

Ever since that day, I have looked upon all living things in a new light. I humbly dedicate this book to its author, The Tree.

Books and music by Dana Lyons available at
www.danalyons.com

BOOKS

Cows With Guns – Illustrated by Jeff Sinclair
The Tree – Illustrated by David Danioth

CD'S & Tapes

Cows with Guns
At Night They Howl at the Moon: Environmental Songs for Kids,
with John Seed (Featuring the song, *The Tree*)
Turn of the Wrench
Animal
Our State is a Dumpsite
Circle the World (with Jane Goodall)
Ride the Lawn.

About the Pacific Rain Forest

Rain forests are one of the most important ecosystems on our planet. They provide homes to more species of plants and animals per square foot than any other habitat in the world. These vital bioregions also replenish our air supply and clean our water. In these nourishing places, we are able to feel the spirit of the earth.

When we think of rain forests, we usually envision a tropical climate — hot, humid jungles with lush, broadleaf plants and trees, monkeys, lizards, brightly feathered birds and other exotic creatures. But the Pacific Rain Forest depicted in *The Tree* is a *temperate* rain forest that stretches along the coast of North America from Southern Oregon to the Gulf of Alaska.

Weather in this region is cool and wet. Yearly rainfall in some places averages 200 inches, equaling more than two billion gallons of water per square mile — 90% of which falls between September and May. Trees growing here are mostly cone-bearing, or *coniferous*, such as the Douglas fir featured in this book. With needles that gather moisture from the fog, they actually create their own "rain." These giants can reach over 300 feet in height and hold more than 5,000 gallons of water.

Able to live well over 800 years, Douglas firs gradually decompose after falling to the forest floor, becoming hosts to thousands of other plants and animals. This process may last as long as it took the tree to grow. Though we could build six houses from just one of these magnificent giants, by protecting them we protect the lives of billions of plants and animals, including mankind.

In *The Tree*, the artist has depicted two authentic totems created by Native Americans who lived in the forest hundreds of years ago. His illustrations include several species that depend upon the Pacific Rain Forest, some of which are in danger of disappearing altogether:

Raven, Bald Eagle, Mouse, Tree Frog, Salmon, Spotted Owl, Timber Wolf, Dragonfly, Cougar, Squirrel, Roosevelt Elk, GrizzlyBear, Bark Beetle, Butterfly, Ladybug, Blacktail Deer, Marten, Banana Slug and *Human.* Can you find them all?

ILLUMINATION
Arts

PUBLISHING COMPANY, INC.
P.O. Box 1865, Bellevue, WA 98009
Tel: 425-644-7185 ★ 888-210-8216 (orders only) ★ Fax: 425-644-9274
liteinfo@illumin.com ★ www.illumin.com

Library of Congress Cataloging-in-Publication Data

Lyons, Dana.
  The tree / Dana Lyons ; David Lane Danioth, illustrator.
    p. cm.
  Summary: An 800-year-old Douglas fir ponders the many things it has seen in the
natural world as it hears the bulldozers coming, and then some people arrive to save it from destruction.
  ISBN 0-9701907-1-9
    [1. Douglas fir—Fiction. 2. Trees—Fiction. 3. Nature—Fiction. 4. Environmental protection—Fiction. 5.
Stories in rhyme.] I. Danioth, David Lane, 1956-, ill. II. Title.
PZ8.3.L98937 Tr 2002
[E]—dc21   2001051472

Third Printing 2006
Published in the United States of America
Printed in Singapore by Tien Wah Press
Book Designer: Molly Murrah, Murrah & Company, Kirkland, WA

Endpapers created by artisan, Ross Cowman, using needles and
seed cones dropped by an 800-year-old Douglas fir.

ILLUMINATION ARTS PUBLISHING COMPANY, INC.
is a member of Publishers in Partnership – replanting our nation's forests.

This book was printed on totally chlorine-free Grycksbo Matte Art Paper (FSC Certified).

More inspiring picture books from Illumination Arts

Little Yellow Pear Tomatoes
Demian Elainé Yumei/Nicole Tamarin, ISBN 0-9740190-2-X
Ponder the never-ending circle of life through the eyes of a young girl, who marvels at all the energy and collaboration it takes to grow yellow pear tomatoes.

Something Special
Terri Cohlene/Doug Keith, ISBN 0-9740190-1-1
A curious little frog finds a mysterious gift outside his home near the castle moat. It's *Something Special*…What can it be?

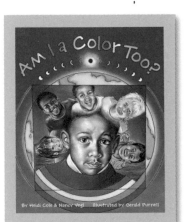

Am I a Color Too?
Heidi Cole/Nancy Vogl/Gerald Purnell, ISBN 0-9740190-5-4
A young interracial boy wonders why people are labeled by the color of their skin. Seeing that people dream, feel, sing, dance and love regardless of their color, he asks, "Am I a color, too?"

Your Father Forever
Travis Griffith/Raquel Abreu, ISBN 0-9740190-3-8

A devoted father promises to nurture, guide, protect and respect his beloved children. This heartwarming poem transcends the boundaries of culture and time in expressing a parent's universal love.

Too Many Murkles
Heidi Charissa Schmidt/Mary Gregg Byrne, ISBN 0-9701907-7-8
Each spring the people of Summerville gather to prevent the dreaded Murkles from entering their village. Unfortunately, this year there are more of the strange, smelly creatures than ever.

We Share One World
Jane E. Hoffelt/Marty Husted, ISBN 0-9701907-8-6
Wherever we live—whether we work in the fields, the waterways, the mountains or the cities—all people and creatures share one world.

In Every Moon There Is A Face
Charles Mathes/Arlene Graston, ISBN 0-9701907-4-3
On this magical voyage of discovery and delight, children of all ages connect with their deepest creative selves.

A Mother's Promise
Lisa Humphrey/David Danioth ISBN 0-9701907-9-4
A lifetime of sharing begins with the sacred vow a woman makes to her unborn child.

To view our whole collection visit us at www.illumin.com